PRISONERS OF THE
BLACK OCTOPUS

This edition first published in 2014 by Book House

© 2015 The Salariya Book Company Ltd

Distributed by Black Rabbit Books
P.O. Box 3263
Mankato
Minnesota MN 56002

First published in France by Éditions Flammarion MMVII

Copyright text and illustration © Éditions Flammarion MMVII

The right of Alain Surget to be identified as the author of this work and the
right of Annette Marnat to be identified as the illustrator of this work has been
asserted in accordance with sections 77 and 78 of the Copyright, Designs and
Patents Act, 1988.

English edition © The Salariya Book Company
& Bailey Publishing Associates MMXI

Translated by Charlotte Coombe

Editor: Shirley Willis

Printed in the United States of America.
Printed on paper from sustainable forests.

Cataloging-in-Publication Data is available
from the Library of Congress

ISBN: 978-1-909645-45-5

The text for this book is set in 1Stone Serif
The display types are set in OldClaude

Written by
Alain Surget

Illustrated by
Annette Marnat

PRISONERS OF THE
BLACK OCTOPUS

Translated by
Charlotte Coombe

BOOK HOUSE

Chapter I

Daylight dawns

Around 1660, in the Caribbean Sea, 130 nautical miles east of Nicaragua.

The sea mirrored the rising sun. The water glowed red with thousands of golden reflections shimmering in it. It was as if the sun had been sprinkled over the tips of the waves. The *Angry Flea* and the *Capricious* sailed into the sunrise, their sails unfurled like great golden-winged albatrosses. Louise and Benjamin were sitting on a lookout platform at the top of the main mast, watching the men below on deck.

"Mending all these torn sails has given me sore fingers," grumbled Louise.

"Me too," said her brother. "We've been slaving away ever since we left Veracruz. These needles are huge!"

"Father's got a funny way of thanking us for

saving his life! I was hoping he'd make us his first mates. I can just see myself with a sword tucked into my belt, shouting out orders!"

"And I thought I'd have my head buried in the charts, working out our course!" added Benjamin.

"I thought we'd both become famous sea captains," said Louise dreamily. "Instead, father's made friends with Parabas and has given him control of the ship."

"But Parabas betrayed him," Benjamin grumbled. "I don't understand why father would trust him again."

"Or why he'd reject us," added Louise bitterly. "Seems like we're no more important to him than the rest of the crew. Look at him down there, leaning on the ship's rail beside Parabas. I wonder what they're plotting."

"Hmmph! Last time we heard what they were saying, they were discussing how to get rid of us."

"Yes," said Louise, nodding. "Ever since that day, I've slept with one eye open."

"Well, I've managed to steal this from the galley,"

whispered Benjamin, lowering his voice as if he was afraid that the wind had ears.

He showed her the knife he'd hidden in his waistband.

"I keep thinking that maybe Cap'n Roc isn't our father," continued Louise.

"Red Mary would know, wouldn't she? She's our sister, she must know our father."

Louise pouted and stuck out her lip—she had no idea.

"I get the feeling that everyone on this ship is lying to us. But why?"

There was no answer. She looked round and saw the *Capricious* bobbing along in the wake of the *Angry Flea*. The ship's single mast made her look like a shark's fin.

"If they'd wanted to throw us into the sea, they would've done it a long time ago," said Benjamin.

Louise leaned against the mast, clasped her hands behind her head, and let out a long sigh.

"I think they need us," continued Benjamin.

"To attack a galleon stuffed full of gold?" Louise scoffed.

"Something else, I'm afraid! What will they do with the treasure once they get their hands on it?" he asked with a solemn expression.

"Bury it in a secret place. Like all pirates do."

"I read somewhere that they kill a sailor and bury him with the chest. The dead man is supposed to guard the treasure."

"So?"

"One half for Cap'n Roc and one half for Parabas. That makes two. And there's two of us!" explained Benjamin. "What if they've decided to sacrifice us for..."

"What nonsense!" said Louise, nudging him

with her elbow. "All that reading's gone to your head. You need to go and scrub the decks and wash thoughts like that away!"

"But..."

"What about Mary, then? You've forgotten her share! Who would she leave at the bottom of the hole? Her uncle? Malibu? Shut-your-trap!?"

A sudden squawk came from the sail above them: "Rrrouououou!"

The children looked up and saw the parrot Shut-your-trap! perched on a rope. He was looking at them with a big beady eye and making deep throaty sounds at them.

A streak of white suddenly flashed past between Louise and the rigging, ruffling her hair as it went.

"What was...?"

"It's a seagull!" said Benjamin.

"A seagull! Then we must be getting near..."

"Land ahoy!" squawked Shut-your-trap! like a cockerel crowing at dawn. "Get yourr violins out! Therrre'll be dancing in the taverrrns tonight, son of a sharrrk!"

Captain Roc's orders were being shouted from one end of the *Angry Flea* to the other.

"Head for shore! Bring the ship about! All hands on deck!"

The helmsman spun the ship's wheel and turned the helm to port, while the rest of the crew let out the ropes to position the sails. The *Angry Flea* creaked loudly as she turned. The wind was now behind her.

"That's Providencia Island," announced Captain Roc.

"There'll be nothing but Indian fishermen on that island," said Parabas.

"And there's a small port full of ex-pirates. The Spanish have lost all interest in it. There are no riches to be found there, so it's not one of their ports of call. We'll stop there to stock up on water, food, gunpowder, and medicines."

"We also need some more men to make up our crew," said Parabas. "We can't attempt to seize gold from the Spanish unless we've got at least 50 men between both our ships."

"We're cunning enough to get our hands on the Incan treasure, but you're right, a few more men wouldn't go amiss. Where are Louise and Benjamin?"

"Still nesting up on their perch."

"They're acting very strangely. They've crossed oceans and faced great danger in search of me, but ever since we've finally found each other, I've had the feeling they've been avoiding me."

"I wonder what they were expecting?"

Captain Roc frowned but didn't say anything.

"We'd better get them down from there," he said. "Because this is where they leave us!"

Chapter II

Providencia Island

As they approached the island, seagulls flocked around them. Dozens of them were landing on the yards and the rigging, getting in the way of the pirates as they hoisted the sails. Their cries drowned out the orders of On-the-Fence, Parabas' first mate who was now in charge of the ship's crew.

"Away with you! Cabin boys! Tenderrrfoots! Time-wasterrrs!" Shut-your-trap! shrieked at the noisy rabble of seagulls that had swooped in on them.

The *Angry Flea* and the *Capricious* glided into the port, where a few fishing boats bobbed about in the water. They drew up alongside the wooden pontoon at the dockside. Two warehouses stood facing out to sea. Behind them, the village spread out in the shape of a crow's foot and was surrounded on all sides by thick forest. Log cabins nestled, higgledy-piggledy, around a small church. There appeared to be as many taverns as there were houses.

"I bet father won't let us go ashore... he'll say it's no place for children!" moaned Louise, who had come back down onto the deck with her brother.

Benjamin looked at the faces of the people who had gathered to watch their ship come in. They were the faces of pirates and ruffians; misshapen and with scruffy beards and whiskers.

"What a rough lot!" said Louise. "We'd better not get on anyone's nerves around here. Even the women look as if they're no stranger to a fight!"

"Yes, I bet even the priest carries a sword," added Benjamin. "You wouldn't want to mess with any of them."

"Benjamin! Louise! Come on, we're going ashore!" cried Captain Roc.

Louise couldn't believe her ears. She turned to her brother, her eyes shining with excitement, and cried:

"Wow! A bit of adventure at last! After all this waiting around on the ship for days on end!"

Benjamin gulped. He'd had quite enough of adventure. All he wanted now was some peace and quiet to read his books, but he was afraid to admit it. He didn't want to be teased and called a landlubber by the rest of the crew or to disappoint his father. So he followed his sister and headed for the gangway.

"Hang on!" cried Captain Roc as Benjamin walked past.

He took off his big hat and placed it on his son's head. Just then, Shut-your-trap! swooped down from the mast and landed on Benjamin's shoulder.

"Perfect!" chuckled Captain Roc. "Now you look like a real pirate!"

"What about me?" cried Louise. "What are you going to give me?"

"I've still got an embroidered handkerchief that belonged to your mother," he replied. "If you want that, I could..."

"I want something from you! Like one of your pistols or something!"

"Fancy that!" he cried.

"Why don't you just ask for the whole ship while you're at it?" said Parabas. "A sewing kit is what you need to put you in your place!"

"I'll make you eat your words!" Louise said threateningly. "Just give me a sword and I'll..."

"Come on, let's go," interrupted her father, placing a hand firmly on her shoulder and guiding her down the gangway. "We've got another Red Mary on our hands here," he said to Parabas.

Louise shrugged him off angrily. Her big sister and the Indian, Tepos, were already waiting on the pontoon. Mary was armed to the teeth with cutlasses, as if she was about to board a ship, and Tepos was leaning on a long rifle. They went ashore, leaving On-the-Fence guarding the *Angry Flea* and Malibu guarding the *Capricious*.

"You two will look after the supplies and weapons," Captain Roc ordered Parabas and Tepos. "Mary and I are in charge of the men."

"And what about us?" asked Louise. "Do we just go off and look around the bird market?"

"Walk right behind us and stay very close," warned Mary as they pushed their way through a crowd of curious onlookers.

"Is this place dangerous?" asked Benjamin, aware of everyone staring at them.

"Forrr surrre!" screeched Shut-your-trap! poking his head out from under the big hat. "They'll make mincemeat out of wimps like you!"

"And they'll have roasted parrot to eat with it!" replied Benjamin.

"Rrrouououou!" cried the bird, disappearing back under the hat.

The narrow streets were packed full of men and donkeys. Goods were being sold in doorways. The streets echoed with the constant racket of people shouting and calling out in a variety of different languages—Arawak, Spanish, and Carib, with a sprinkling of English, Dutch, and French. There was a strong scent of vanilla in the air, a heady smell that masked the odor of dung and the whiff of grilled fish. Bunches of black vanilla pods hung from the walls of the houses and around the doors, as if the inhabitants were not just drying them out, but were also trying to use them to ward off evil spirits. The taverns rang with the sound of laughter and sudden brawls. Indians who had once been great warriors with feathered headdresses were now sitting in doorways in dusty rags like beggars.

"Are you taking us to The Black Octopus?" asked Red Mary.

"Yes. That's where we'll find the right sort of crowd."

"The Black Octopus?" repeated the bird, digging its claws into Benjamin's shoulder. "Billy goat's horrrn! It'll all kick off in therrre!"

"He seems to know the place well," said Benjamin in a slightly strangled tone of voice as he felt a knot beginning to form in his stomach.

Louise's face lit up in a smile and she started leaping around as if attacking an invisible enemy.

"Give me that!" she said, grabbing the hat from her brother. "You've got the parrot, that's all you need! It's better if they don't realize I'm a girl," she added, before he could protest. "Luckily I dumped my dress in the bushes ages ago!"

"You're going to get into real trouble, you know."

"I'll be the one causing it, more like," she corrected him, shaking her fist. "Oh! How I'd love to get Parabas by the throat! Or I could knock out a couple of pirates instead and just pretend it was him."

They came to an enormous tree covered in red flamelike flowers. It stood in front of a squat building with a balcony. Nailed to the tree trunk was a wooden sign for The Black Octopus—carved with a terrifying octopus grappling with a ship. Suddenly they heard shouting, an angry outburst, and the sound of breaking glass. A man came flying through the window and landed at Red Mary's feet. She gave him a mighty kick and he slumped to the ground, sprawled on his stomach. He turned his head with an angry scowl, but his expression changed when he saw the young woman and Captain Roc. He leaped to his feet and fled down the nearest alleyway. Watching this scene unfold, Louise puffed out her chest with self-importance and was ready to follow her sister into the tavern when her father grabbed her arm.

"You two—wait outside!"

"What?" spluttered Louise. "You've brought us all the way here just to leave us outside the door? You might as well have left us on the ship!"

"We'll keep watch," said Benjamin, relieved at not having to go inside the pirates' den.

"Good idea," said Captain Roc. "But I forbid you

to go more than twenty paces from this tree!" he said sternly, looking straight at Louise.

Louise sat down sulkily on the ground, with her elbows resting on her knees. Her brother sat down next to her and leaned his back against the wall.

Shut-your-trap! was perched on a branch overhead. A moment later, Louise jumped up again, with a mischievous look on her face.

"Where are you going?" Benjamin asked as she headed for the flame tree.

"I'm getting rusty sitting here. I'm just going to stretch my legs a bit."

"But... father said..."

"Don't worry, I won't go more than twenty paces from the tree trunk. Come over here—I need your help."

Benjamin went across to join her under a low branch. She told him to cup his hands together so she could use them as a step to climb up onto his shoulders.

"Trrrramplerrr! Crrrusherrr! Squasherrr!" squawked Shut-your-trap! He had toppled off his perch on Benjamin's shoulder and flown up to sit on a nearby branch.

Louise climbed up and grabbed hold of a branch. She hung from it and after swinging three times, managed to wrap her legs around it.

"There we go!" she said triumphantly, sitting upright on the branch. "The rest is easy!"

"The rest? The rest of what?" muttered Benjamin, who had finally realized, too late, what his sister had in mind. "What are you planning to do?"

"Get inside The Black Octopus, of course!"

"Cap'n Rrroc will hang you frrrom the highest yarrrd of the ship!" Shut-your-trap! screeched from his perch beside her. "It'll be a jolly sight, son of a sharrrk!"

"Hey, you! I'll stuff you inside my hat if you don't keep your beak shut! Got it? Son of a doggg!" she retorted, in the same tone of voice as the parrot.

"Oh, no!" muttered Benjamin in despair, as Louise carried on climbing up the tree. "This will end in disaster."

She disappeared among the mass of flowers and her voice could only just be heard through the rustling of the leaves:

"Don't worry! Father won't see me!"

The parrot came back to perch on Benjamin's shoulder again.

"Rrrououou..."

"You said it," sighed Benjamin. "You said it..."

Chapter III

At The
Black Octopus

Everyone in the tavern fell silent as Captain Roc and Red Mary walked in. The gambler who had just hurled his opponent out of the window sat back down again, frowned, and started shuffling his cards. Men sat slumped at tables, pipes hanging from their mouths, three-cornered hats rammed onto their heads, their eyes fixed on the two new arrivals. Every single one of them had heard of the famous pirate and his daughter. Those who'd already had a brush with them in the past pulled their hats down farther and tried to hide their faces with their hands. Others just shook their heads and buried their noses in their jars of rum or brandy. Captain Roc looked slowly around the smoke-filled room, looking for someone in particular.

"Ah!" he said, noticing an old man with a wooden leg.

He went over to him. The old pirate moved his peg leg out of Captain Roc's way and raised a pewter tankard to toast the captain's health. Captain Roc gave him a pat on the shoulder.

"How are you, Spring-leg?"

The old pirate squinted at him, and gave a wide, toothless grin.

"What brings you two to Providencia?" he rasped in a husky voice. "What a surprise to see father and daughter together again."

"Let us sit down," said Captain Roc, prodding him lightly.

The old man shuffled along the bench. Mary sat down next to him. Her father took a stool from a nearby table and sat down opposite Spring-leg. He called to a girl in a red dress who was busy serving customers.

"Hey, gorgeous! Bring us a tall jug of rum!"

The girl hurried to serve them as the rest of the tavern carried on talking among themselves.

"So, what does brings you to Providencia?" Spring-leg asked again, after glugging down his rum.

Captain Roc beckoned him closer and leaned across the table.

"I've lost most of my crew. But there must be pirates on this island who are looking for adventure."

Spring-leg grimaced, partly because his tankard was empty again and partly out of suspicion.

"You always seem to be losing your crew," he said. "Either at the bottom of the sea or hanging from the gallows."

"There will be a lot of gold in it," Captain Roc assured him, lowering his voice.

"Yes, for you, no doubt. But what about your men?"

Mary refilled their jars as her father continued:

"The Spanish have taken Incan gold on board at Cartagena. And it's just waiting to change hands... That galleon is carrying more treasure than any man could collect in a lifetime of pillaging, and there's enough for everyone," he added emphatically.

Spring-leg knocked back some more rum and clicked his tongue.

"Even if you did find any madmen to go with you, do you plan to storm the galleon with just the *Marie-Louise*? There will surely be a whole armada of ships escorting this Spanish galleon!"

"The *Marie-Louise* was destroyed in Mayan country. I'm sailing on the *Angry Flea* now."

"That's Black Beard's ship!" spluttered the old

man. Suddenly all eyes were on them. "Did you beat that rascal?"

"None of your business!" said Mary impatiently. "The *Capricious* will be going into battle, too. She's quicker than a frigate and easier to handle. She can slip between the escort ships and her cannons can do serious damage, too. But father and I need more men to storm the ship."

Spring-leg stuck his lip out and made a low growling sound at the back of his throat, as if he was thinking hard.

"Hmmm... Sounds like you need Windbag's band of pirates."

"Who's that?" asked Captain Roc.

"He's a deserter from the British navy who's taken to piracy. He arrived on the island not long ago, but the swine has already attracted the most ugly, despicable band of pirates ever to walk the earth. He's a real gallows bird who would sell his own mother and father for a handful of peanuts."

"Why's he called Windbag?" asked Mary, puzzled.

"Ever since he was shot in the jaw he hasn't been able to shut his mouth properly. He looks like he's swallowing the wind and anything in it, like a nighthawk. But it certainly doesn't stop him from squealing like a stuck pig. Beware of him though!" warned the old pirate. "That scoundrel is just as likely to stir up a mutiny on board, just to get his hands on your ship."

"But not before we've robbed the Spanish of their gold!" quipped Captain Roc.

"It's no laughing matter! The last time he boarded a ship, he threw the captain to the sharks!"

"That's a risk I'm willing to take!" said Captain Roc, slamming his jar down on the table. "Where can I find this...?"

Just then a huge crash came from the back room, quickly followed by a sound like a wolf howling and then a tirade of loud angry cursing.

"Hear that?" said Spring-leg. "That's Windbag shrieking back there. I wouldn't want to be the one who..."

A clear, shrill voice now carried through from

the back room. It cut through the noise of the tavern like the blade of a sword.

"Hah?" said Mary, jumping to her feet. "That sounds like Louise!"

Chapter IV

Windbag

Moments earlier, just as her father and sister were sitting down at Spring-leg's table, Louise had reached a branch of the flame tree that was level with the balcony. She was used to climbing the ship's rigging and in no time at all she had shimmied along the branch, positioned herself opposite the balcony railings, and leapt across the gap. She clung to the balcony, swung her leg over and pushed open the French windows. Shut-your-trap! shot off Benjamin's shoulder and swooped into the room after Louise.

In the room there was a bed, a chest of drawers, a trunk, and chairs in three of the corners. It was a lady's room, judging by the brushes and bottles strewn across the dressing table and the large tilting

mirror standing next to the bed, opposite the lamp. Shut-your-trap! flew across to perch on the mirror, but it wobbled as he landed, giving him such a fright that he almost toppled off.

"All hands on deck! The enemy's aboarrrd! All hands on... Squawk!"

A hand clutched him by the throat and the parrot couldn't get the last words out.

"One more squawk out of you and I swear I'll throttle you!" Louise threatened him.

"Rrr...!"

She stuffed him inside her hat and wedged it under her arm to keep the bird quiet. She opened the door a sliver. "What with all that noise downstairs, I don't suppose anyone would've heard the stupid creature," she decided. "I'll risk going out into the corridor."

The corridor was just a wooden platform above a room downstairs, with a rickety banister leading to the bottom of the staircase. "This must be the back room," thought Louise. "I can't see father or Mary. I'll go downstairs. I'd be very surprised if anyone notices me among all these folk." Still clutching Shut-your-trap! inside her hat, Louise had just started edging along the balcony when a door opened behind her. Turning around, she came face to face with a fat, barrel-chested man with a mustache.

"What on earth are you doing here?" he roared. "I don't know you! What's that you've got under your arm?"

"My hat," she replied, catching sight of some buckets of water through the half-opened door.

"You're hiding something in that hat. You've pinched things from the bedrooms!"

"I'm not a thief!" she snorted indignantly, moving back toward the stairs.

His huge hand made a grab for her.

"Show me what you're hiding in there!"

As he snatched the hat, Shut-your-trap! shot out, startling the man. Louise took the opportunity to grab his sword. As she did so, she slashed his waistband. His pants fell down around his ankles.

"Hey!" he cried. "What the devil? Just wait 'til I get my hands on you..."

He said no more. The parrot, flapping his wings, lunged at the man's face, blocking his way.

"Open the gunporrrts!" he screeched. "Cannons, take aim! It's all kicking off, son of a sharrrk!"

Louise put her head down and charged at the huge man, hitting him square in the belly. He staggered backward and bumped into the banister. He tried to keep his balance but, with his pants still round his ankles, he tripped and fell over the edge. He landed on the floor below, right in the middle of the table where Windbag was sitting. Windbag fell flat on his back with a bottle of rum and the enormous man on his lap. He let out a howl of rage followed by a stream of curses. He shoved the big-bellied man off, ready for a fight.

"It was that girl up there!" the man yelled, pointing at Louise. "She was upstairs snooping about in the bedrooms!"

Windbag stood up. The entire room turned to stare at Louise, who was standing at the top of

the stairs with a big hat on her head and a sword clasped in her hand. The crowd started to laugh, but not Windbag. He drew his long sword and stepped onto the bottom of the staircase.

"There's a law on this island," he said. "We don't steal from fellow Brothers of the Coast. You seem to have forgotten that, you little runt!"

"I didn't steal anything," Louise protested. "But if it's a fight you want, I'm ready and waiting for you, Twisted Face!"

"This little birdie obviously doesn't know who she's speaking to," muttered Windbag. "I'll make her swallow her sword!"

Flourishing his sword, he rushed up the stairs. Shut-your-trap! panicked and started flapping around the room, screeching out in a shrill voice:

"Save yourrrselves! Man the lifeboats! Abandon ship!"

As Windbag reached the top of the stairs, Louise squared up to him, her eyes burning defiantly, her teeth gritted. She was the first to launch the attack. Their swords clashed as they twirled around. With one swift move, Windbag sent Louise's sword flying into the air.

She found herself cornered, her back to the wall.

"And now..." he cried.

Suddenly, he felt his hat being whipped off and heard the sound of a blade striking wood. Flabbergasted, he saw his three-cornered hat pinned to the wall, the knife handle still vibrating.

"Get your hands off my sister!" came a voice from behind him.

Everyone turned to see who it was. A name was whispered around the room.

"Red Mary?" said Windbag in surprise, repeating the name he had just heard. "And who is Red Mary?"

"She's my daughter!" thundered Captain Roc, appearing behind him. "And so is that little birdie you were about to do away with!"

"And who are you? You owe me a hat, by the way!"

"You can have a boat full of them if you agree to bring your men and join my crew."

"And whose crew might that be, then?"

"They call me Cap'n Roc."

"Cap'n Roc..." replied the pirate, as if grinding the words between his teeth. "I've heard a lot about you. The Spanish and the English would pay a lot of money for your capture."

"And yours. The equivalent of a herd of cows, I believe."

"We're at the mercy of jealous men," said Windbag, slowly making his way back downstairs.

"So let's sit down with a jug of rum and talk," suggested Captain Roc. "And as for you, I told you to wait outside for us!" he said to Louise.

Windbag exchanged a knowing look with some of his accomplices in the room. He smiled, nodded, and shook Captain Roc's hand.

"Very well," he said, "as long as you give the gold doubloons... to me!" he cried, suddenly grabbing hold of the captain's hand.

Instantly, there was a scuffle of chairs and four ruffians leaped toward Mary and her father. Two of them jumped on Mary while the others squared up to Captain Roc.

"I only sell my services to whoever is the strongest," said Windbag, pushing the tip of his sword up against Captain Roc's throat. "You're more valuable dead than alive, it seems. I could buy my freedom back by handing your dead body over to..."

"Hey! Twisted Face!" yelled Louise.

No sooner had he turned his head, than he caught sight of a bucket flying toward him.

"What the...?"

The wooden bucket clattered to the floor by his feet, splashing him waist-high with water. Everyone instinctively took a step backward. Captain Roc shook his arm free.

"Take coverrr!" warned Shut-your-trap! as another bucket of water flew through the air.

This time it struck the shoulder of one of the pirates who was holding Captain Roc. Seizing the moment, Captain Roc punched the other pirate in the jaw and hurled him toward Windbag, before rushing over to Mary to free her from the other two pirates. Windbag's gang were all knocked to the ground by the attack.

Just then, Spring-leg's rasping voice hollered out: "A triple tot of rum to anyone who gets out of here on two legs!"

Everyone suddenly leaped to their feet, jumping over benches and tables. All at once a free-for-all broke out, a real dog-fight. Punches swung in all directions, at anyone and everyone. It didn't matter who as long as they hit someone. The serving girls rushed to take shelter in the main room, but were pushed back into the brawl by other ruffians flocking to join in.

Benjamin had run into the tavern when he heard the first shouts. He found himself being dragged into the crowd. No sooner had he entered the back room when, out of the blue, he was hit on the head by a jug. He tried to shelter under a nearby table.

The pirates fought with the same gusto as they made merry—with all their hearts. They broke chairs, smashed jars, spilled drinks, and threw the pewter tankards about. They shouted and chuckled as they settled old scores. Mary knocked out one of the pirates who had grabbed her, and was chasing the other around a table, while her father shoved Windbag's nose into a puddle of wine. Alongside him, Louise showered her opponents with water from a large bucket that the fat man used as a bathtub.

"Firrre on the porrrt side! Firrre on the starrrboarrrd

side!" cried Shut-your-trap! as he flapped around above the ruckus. "Reload the..."

BANG!

An explosion stopped everyone in their tracks. Shut-your-trap! almost dropped out of the air with fright, but, flapping his wings madly, he reached a perch on the banister.

"That's enough, you gang of savages!" screamed a woman's voice.

A fearsome, hard-faced woman with black hair stood there, pointing an enormous blunderbuss, the gun's mouth gaping like a great crater.

"I've just loaded it," she snarled. "And I'll blow the first person that moves to kingdom come, as sure as my name is Carla Dominga! Every single one of you will leave me two coins on your way out. That'll pay for the damage."

Everyone did as they were told, each dropping small coins into a bowl as they filed out one by one. As Red Mary was about to leave her share, she said to Carla Dominga:

"It was my sister who started all this trouble at your tavern. I'll leave her here along with her brother to help you tidy up."

"No!" protested Louise. "Without me, Twisted Face would've torn father and you to pieces!"

"An excellent idea," agreed Captain Roc. "I need

to find Windbag, we've got unfinished business. But I'll come straight back afterward."

Louise tried to follow her father, but Carla Dominga grabbed her by the shoulders and held her back.

"Stay here, little chicken! And you, too!" she added, blocking Benjamin's way with her huge gun.

"Oh!" said Mary, just as she was about to leave. "I'll have my knife back."

She reached out to Louise's waistband and grabbed the knife that had pinned Windbag's three-cornered hat to the wall. Then, with a sly half-smile, she raised her hand in a small farewell gesture.

"Father's abandoning us," whispered Louise.

"No, he's not," Benjamin replied. "He said he'd come back for us."

But Benjamin didn't sound too sure, as if he doubted his own words. "Perhaps he really does want to get rid of us," he thought. "And he's decided to dump us here."

Chapter V

Abandoned!

It was not long before the back room of The Black Octopus looked like a tavern again. All the tables had been righted, all the sword nicks in the furniture had been filled with wax, and the broken chairs had been stacked up in a corner. The two children were just finishing off sweeping the floor. They were being helped by a serving girl called Marina, a huge Indian woman with plaits as thick as snakes that reached down to her waist.

"Father's taking his time coming back," grumbled Louise.

"It obviously took him longer than he thought to persuade those men to join his crew."

"As if!" she scoffed. "As soon as they hear the word 'gold,' even the one-legged men will be galloping toward the ships."

"Anyway, as soon as we're finished here, the landlady will let us go. All we've got left to do is..."

Benjamin fell silent as he heard Carla Dominga say: "Oh! About time, too!" Then they heard Captain Roc's voice in the next room.

"To hell with The Black Octopus!" trilled Louise, throwing her broom to the floor with a clatter. "We're going back aboard the *Angry Flea*!"

"We'rrre casting off!" shouted Benjamin, imitating Shut-your-trap!, and he hurled his broom across the room, too.

The broom crashed into a large, beautiful stoneware jug that sat on a nearby table—the only jug that had survived the pirates' brawl—and smashed it. With surprising agility, Marina quickly wedged her huge body into the archway between the two rooms, blocking their way.

"Hey, kid! You break, you mend!" she said in a mixture of broken French and Spanish.

"Let us through!"

Marina shook her head.

"Father's come back to get us," explained

Benjamin. "You can't make us stay here because of an old jug."

Marina, as unflinching as a rock, did not move an inch.

"She's as stubborn as a mule," said Louise. "Father! Father!" she yelled.

There was no reply. Yet they could hear their father talking to Carla Dominga. Benjamin started to call out as well.

"You break, you mend," insisted Marina.

Louise flopped down with a grumpy look on her face and folded her arms, absolutely refusing to pick up her broom.

"Just you wait and see," she said sulkily. "When we come back with a ship's hold stuffed full of gold, I'll take you on as my maid and make you sweep the decks with your plaits!"

They heard Captain Roc's voice again next door, and then it got fainter. The door clicked shut and silence fell. The children were astounded.

"I... I don't believe it!" stuttered Benjamin. "Father's left without us."

After a moment of shock, Louise threw herself at
Marina, hitting out with her fists to try and make
her budge, shouting:

"Father! Father!"

Marina put her arm around Louise and lifted her
off the floor. Then, turning on her heel, she picked

up Benjamin, who was trying to slip between her and the wall. With both of them under her arms like sacks of flour, Marina took them into the middle of the room and set them down on a bench, without letting go of them. Carla Dominga came in and stood in front of them, hands on hips. Then she told them:

"Cap'n Roc sets sail tonight, and he doesn't want any little mosquitoes getting under his feet!"

"Mosquitoes?" spluttered Louise indignantly. "But we're his children!"

"If he's worried that we'll get in the way, we can stay up the main mast or in the cabin," added Benjamin.

"I know how to haul down a sail and tie a halyard to a cleat," protested Louise. "We're useful on a ship, my brother and I."

"You don't seem to understand," the woman said, placing her hands flat on the table and leaning toward them. "Your father's decided to get rid of you."

"That's not true!" cried Louise, standing bolt upright.

Marina pushed her down again.

"Exactly what did he tell you? What?" said Louise, punching and kicking the table angrily.

"He said that you should stay here at The Black Octopus. Both of you." said Carla Dominga sternly.

Hearing this, Louise began to tremble.

"Father has... sold us off!" she sobbed.

Benjamin put his arms around his sister and hugged her.

"Calm down, Louise, calm down," he pleaded.

He put his mouth close to her ear and whispered:

"We'll get out of here, I promise. I've still got that kitchen knife I stole from the *Angry Flea*."

Louise sniffed and took in several deep gulps of air to help her breathe normally again. Her heart stopped pounding and her body relaxed. She sat very still with her chest leaning against the edge of the table, feeling overwhelmed.

"You have a choice, little cabin boys," said Carla Dominga. "Either you carry out the jobs I give you properly, or I lock you in the cellar with the barrels."

"All right," sighed Benjamin. "We'll do what you ask."

"So get to work then! There's still broken glass all over the floor. When you've finished cleaning up this room, go and find the other chairs in the shed and bring them in here. Marina, keep a close eye on these two slippery eels! I forbid you to let them go out before the ships have set sail. I don't want Cap'n Roc firing one of his cannons at my tavern."

Dejectedly, the children got up and went over to pick up their brooms. They started sweeping again,

half–heartedly, like a pair of rag dolls, their minds elsewhere.

"Prisoners," Louise muttered. "We're prisoners here at The Black Octopus."

"Rrrououou…" added Shut-your-trap! from his perch up on the iron chandelier.

Chapter VI

Carla Dominga's revelations

Evening fell and Providencia Island quickly sank into the velvety darkness of night. At The Black Octopus, the customers were drinking rowdily, under the watchful eye of Carla Dominga and her blunderbuss. After a while she left Marina and the other serving girls in charge and went upstairs to the bedrooms. She took down a key that hung on a nail, went to one of the doors, turned the key in the lock, and opened it. Louise and Benjamin were huddled up beneath the window, which had bars on it. They didn't look up at the woman as she entered. Even Shut-your-trap! looked as though he'd shrunk down into his feathers.

"Look at your faces, both of you!" exclaimed Carla Dominga. She took Louise's chin in her hand

and saw that her face was wet with tears.

It was Benjamin who answered.

"So how would you feel, exactly, if you were us, finding out that your father had abandoned you? We crossed the ocean to find him, we saved him from the clutches of the Spanish, and he's rejected us as if we had the plague. What have we done to deserve this?"

"He hasn't abandoned you."

"He told you to keep us prisoner here!" hissed Louise. "He's going off to sea, and we've just been left here as prisoners in this tavern. He's sold us and disappeared without a word. He's a coward, a traitor, a pig, a... a..."

Carla Dominga pulled up a stool next to her.

"You've got it all wrong," she sighed. "I've known Cap'n Roc for a long time, and I promise you he's not a coward, a traitor, or a pig."

"We overheard father talking to Parabas," Benjamin continued. "He definitely said that he wanted to get rid of us."

"He's not our real father!" said Louise sharply.

"I'm going to keep on dreaming about our real father."

"Come, come," said Carla Dominga, patting her on the shoulder. "Cap'n Roc really is your father, believe me. He only left you behind because he

doesn't want to risk your lives in battle at sea. It's a very dangerous venture. His ship could be sunk. He loves you too much to bear the thought of your getting hurt."

"Is that what he told you?"

"Yes. And he didn't sound like he was lying."

"So why did he leave without saying goodbye?" said Louise. "Why didn't he come and explain that to us himself?"

"Your father's not used to this kind of situation. He knows how to command a crew, but he doesn't know how to deal with his own children. He was afraid of giving in to you, or that he'd have to be very stern to make you stay on the island. It was easier for me to do it."

"We would've liked a hug, all the same," said Benjamin sadly.

"Cap'n Roc doesn't like goodbyes. You can hug him when he gets back."

"Will it be like this every time?" asked Louise.

"This is his last voyage," said Carla Dominga. "Cap'n Roc is tired of sailing the seven seas."

"Really? He's going to stay with us afterward?" said Louise in delight, her eyes shining with hope.

Carla Dominga nodded and smiled.

"At first, he'll be like a big albatross stranded on land. He'll miss life at sea and he'll often be silent. You'll have to be patient with him," she warned

them. "It won't always be easy, for him or for you."

"Why did you lock us up in here instead of just telling us that?" said Benjamin. "And why were you so mean to us?"

"Cap'n Roc told me to keep my eye on you both while he was loading his ship with cargo

and sorting out his new crew, Windbag's pirates. Knowing you, he realized that you would try to get back to the *Angry Flea* or the *Capricious*. That's why I locked you up here at The Black Octopus. And if I've been a bit harsh, let's just put it down to having all my chairs and rum jars smashed. As of tomorrow, you'll be free to roam the island... but I'll still be looking after you," explained Carla Dominga. "Oh," she said, as she got up, "tonight is the night of San Juan. Don't be surprised if you hear lots of shouting and explosions in the streets!"

She went toward the door. As she was leaving, she turned to the children and added:

"Don't worry about your little family! Cap'n Roc will keep them safe from the Spanish cannonballs and all five of you will soon be back together again."

"Five?" said Louise, raising an eyebrow. "But there are only four of us, with father and Mary."

"You're forgetting Roger de Parabas."

"Parabas?" said Benjamin. "What's he got to do with us?"

"He's your father's cousin. Didn't you know?"

The door clicked shut and the key turned in the lock. Louise and her brother were left dumbfounded.

"Parabas... father's cousin? Our cousin? Now I see why father didn't throw him into the ship's hold," said Benjamin.

"Parrrrabas! Parrrabas!" cackled Shut-your-trap! as if the name had suddenly woken him up. "He's crrrazy, Parrrabas, underneath his big ha...!"

Louise whacked him on the head with the hat.

"Don't insult our family!"

"Rrrououou!"

The bird took refuge on top of the chest and began pecking at the wood with his beak.

"Hang on a minute!" exclaimed Benjamin excitedly. "If Parabas is a marquis then that means that father must be a marquis, too. At the very least... or maybe even a duke or a prince?"

"So that means we must be,too!"

But Benjamin's enthusiasm didn't last long.

"Yes, we may be nobles, but we're ruined ones. Remember that Parabas became a pirate to try and get rich again. If father followed the same path, it's likely that he didn't have a penny to his name either. And if mother hadn't worked as a seamstress in Paris, we would have lived in total poverty."

"You're forgetting father's treasure," said Louise, getting carried away. "And the Incan gold that he's going to steal from the Spanish. With that, he'll have enough to buy the Louvre Palace!"

"That's if Parabas and Mary don't steal it all from him. I don't trust either of them."

"You're right," Louise said, her face darkening. "We've got to get back on the *Angry Flea*, to keep an eye on those two. Do you think you could work those bars loose with your knife?"

Benjamin looked closely at the window frame.

"It's made from soft wood," he said, taking a nick out of the windowsill. "It wouldn't take me very long."

"Let's wait till night time, once Carla Dominga has brought our supper," Louise suggested. "With all the celebrations for San Juan going on, no one will notice us outside. I wonder..." she said, lying down on the bed and clasping her hands behind her head.

"What?"

"I was just wondering if Roc is our real surname? Cap'n Roc, that's more like a pirate's name, like Black Beard, Scarface, or One-eyed Jack. But something like Lescure, Rochejacquelein, Rochefoucauld," she said, listing aristocratic names and savoring them like candy. "Mmm... names like that would be more suitable for people like us!"

Chapter VII

The night
of San Juan

The night exploded with noise. It sounded like cannons firing or a battle at sea. But instead, it was fireworks bursting into the sky with sparkling showers of light and the shouts were cries of joy. With the music, singing, and dancing that filled the tavern, The Black Octopus almost seemed to be swaying from side to side in time with all the crazy rhythms.

"Carla Dominga must be sitting in the archway between the rooms with her finger on the trigger, ready to fire her blunderbuss at the slightest sign of trouble," muttered Louise.

"What will we do if father sends us back?" said Benjamin anxiously as he pared wood away from around the bars.

"Hopefully, we can sneak onto the ship under

cover of darkness, and hide in the hold. Once out on the high seas, father isn't going to turn around to bring us back."

"But what if he finds us before then?"

"Oh!" she said in an irritated voice. "We'll just have to wait and see what happens. Hurry up, we still need to tie the sheets together, and the night's almost halfway through already."

Concentrating, with his tongue between his teeth, Benjamin finally loosened the last couple of bars and put the knife back in his waistband. He gripped the bottom of the iron grate, tilted it toward him, gave it a yank, and pulled it free of the wooden window frame. Then he helped his sister tie the sheets together, end to end, and added a blanket that he'd found in a chest.

"That should be long enough," said Louise.

They dragged the bed closer to the window and tied their makeshift rope to one of its legs. Louise grabbed Shut-your-trap! by his neck.

"Not a peep out of you. Not a word. Not even a rrrououou!"

Then she hurled him out of the window. One after the other, Benjamin and Louise used the knotted sheets to clamber down the wall and jumped to the ground.

"We'd better go through the forest," said Benjamin. "Imagine if we bumped into one of the crew or a bunch of drunks!"

Louise agreed. They avoided the main square in front of the church, where the townspeople were running wild. Rum was flowing freely and firecrackers were going off all over the place. The children crept up a back alley that led out of town and into the forest. Keeping to the edge of the woods, they made their way around the little town. Sudden bursts of fireworks lit up the night sky and the air was filled with the smell of gunpowder. Men and women leaped and danced around the bonfire. In the firelight, they looked like burning demons and the scene was like some ancient pagan celebration.

Louise and Benjamin cursed as they tripped over tree roots, fell into waterlogged holes, and had their faces whipped by branches as they ran. They passed the center of the town and then headed for the sea. It was much darker when they reached the port. Torches flashed here and there on the pontoon and the docks, casting light on the pirates who were carrying sacks and kegs toward one of the ships.

"Mary's ship must have set sail already," said Louise. "Father's is taking longer to load."

"That's to be expected—it's a much bigger ship. But how are we going to get aboard now?"

"I've got an idea. Let's get inside two of these sacks! The last sacks to be loaded in the ship's hold will be at the top of the pile. It'll be easy to get out."

The children boldly made their way between the warehouses and waited for the pirates who were loading the sacks to head back to the ship again. When they were sure that the coast was clear, they ran to the cargo stacked on the dockside, picked out two large sacks of lentils, dragged them over to the water's edge and emptied most of the contents into the water. Then they quickly ran back to the rest of the cargo with them.

"Take Shut-your-trap! with you," Benjamin whispered to his sister. "Stuff him inside your hat. That will muffle the sound if he starts squawking!"

"Barrrbarrrians! Savages... arrrggh!"

"Done!" whispered Louise.

She got into one of the sacks with the hat and the parrot clutched tightly under her arm and settled herself among the lentils. Benjamin retied the cord then climbed inside his own sack. As he crouched down, he took one last look at the ship as it swayed gently on the waves.

"The ship looks slightly different," he thought. "It's probably because it's so dark, and I'm seeing it from behind." He settled down into the lentils and tried as best he could to tie the sack shut over his head.

The men returned wearily, dragging their feet with tiredness. They bent down, grabbed the sacks and kegs, and heaved them onto their shoulders.

"Hey!" said one of them in surprise. "This sack isn't even tied up properly. The cap'n would have me whipped if I lost half this stuff on the way to the ship."

He tied up the cord, much to the relief of Benjamin, who had been afraid that the pirate might open the sack to check the goods inside. Once hoisted onto the men's backs, the children kept very still. They could tell by the sound of the footsteps that they had left the stone wharf and were now on the wooden pontoon, then on the gangway and finally onto the deck of the ship. A few words were exchanged and then they were bumped about as the pirates took them through the hatch below deck, down a steep staircase. They were suddenly dropped into the storeroom. They tumbled several yards down before landing on their stomachs with a thud. Benjamin almost choked as his mouth filled with lentils. He heard Shut-your-trap! squawk as Louise fell on top of him, and then the trap door clanked shut.

There was complete silence in the hold—a heavy, almost overwhelming silence that seemed endless. Then came the sound of bare feet running overhead, up on deck. Beams creaked. Then a strange feeling as the ship swayed beneath them. "That's it," sighed Benjamin. "We're off!"

Chapter VIII

In the belly
of the ship

For a while, the ship's hull swayed to and fro. The ship moved forward in fits and starts, as it was sucked downward and then bobbed up again with the rise and fall of the waves. Pirates came down to the hold a couple of times, bringing barrels of water, but it had been a long time now since they had heard anyone.

"Louise," Benjamin whispered.

He heard a muffled reply from his sister.

"I think we can come out now," he said.

He grabbed his knife and ripped the canvas sack open. A stream of lentils poured out. In the blink of an eye, he had hauled himself free of the sack. He quickly cut the cord on the other one to let Louise out. The hat started flapping about.

"Son of a sharrrk, it's as hot and darrrk as an oven!"

They felt their way over the pile of sacks and headed for the trap door that would take them up between decks. They found a staircase, climbed up the steps, and pushed the wooden panel up. In the space above them, a red light was visible through the open hatch—the first glimmer of dawn reflecting off the sea. Hammocks suspended on hooks swung rhythmically above some chests that were nailed to the floor. Cannons were fastened with ropes and positioned at the gunports. Every five paces lanterns hung from the wooden beams to light up the cannons when the area was filled with smoke.

"That's strange," remarked Benjamin. "Something feels different."

"Well obviously, father's taken on a new crew. Parabas' men have had to make room for Twisted Face's... that's my nickname for Windbag."

"How are we going to explain to father why we're here? What shall we tell him?"

"We'll tell him that we love him. That we couldn't bear to be separated from him. That... that... oh, I don't know, I'm sure we'll think of something!"

They were climbing another staircase leading to the upper deck, when suddenly a tall, thin man blocked their way. The children were as surprised as he was.

"Captain!" hollered the beanpole of a pirate in the direction of the poop deck. "I think the Devil's sent us a little gift!"

"I've seen him somewhere before," muttered Louise, with a frown. "But where? It wasn't at The Black Octopus, or on the *Angry Flea* or the *Capricious...*"

"Or at the fortress at Port-Royal," murmured Benjamin. "Maybe it was at Veracruz."

"I've got it!" cried Louise. "He's one of the pirates who took us to St. Malo!"

A terrible laugh rang out behind them.

"Ha ha! It seems the Devil's on our side. Welcome aboard the *Red Hand*, my little pirates!"

That voice! Before they had even looked round, Benjamin and Louise realized they had fallen into the hands of...

"Black Bearrrd! Terrrorrr of the seas! Rrrouououou!" shrieked Shut-your-trap!, vanishing aloft.

"Get up on deck!" boomed Black Beard as the crew gathered around the hatch to look

at the children.

Louise held her brother's hand. Together, they climbed up the last few steps. The tall, thin man grabbed them by their collars and brought them before the frightful pirate, who was leaning on the railing of the poop deck waiting for them, next to an old man with a wooden leg.

"I've been following your father for two days. I lost sight of him tonight, but now I know where he's headed. One of my old friends has told me everything and even wants to serve as one of my pirates again. Isn't that right, Spring-leg?"

The old pirate sniggered.

"The lure of gold eases my old aching bones."

"Cap'n Roc will need my cannons to help him beat the Spanish," Black Beard continued. "Then, in exchange for your lives, I'll demand his hidden treasure and all the loot, too. That'll mean I can buy the island of my dreams, take a wife in high society, and become a respectable sugarcane grower."

"You'll end your days swinging off the end of a rope!" Louise retorted.

The tall, lanky pirate gave them a shove, and asked:

"Shall I lock 'em in the hold?"

"No! They might as well make themselves useful. My coat's missing some buttons and my shoes need polishing. The sails need patching up, ropes need mending, the deck needs a good scrub, and there are rats to catch in the storeroom. And as for the rest of you, don't just stand there gawping. Get back to work, you lazy bunch. Or it'll be the cat-of-nine-tails for you!"

"That's a sort of whip," Benjamin whispered to Louise.

The pirates scurried off back to work.

"Black Beard or not, this ship is still taking us to our father," Louise said. "Let's just do as this rat-eater says for now! And then..."

"And then..." sighed Benjamin. "Who knows what'll happen to us then..."

ABOUT THE AUTHOR

Alain Surget is a professor of history as well as a prolific novelist. He started writing plays and poetry at the early age of 14, then went on to write more than 130 novels and other books. Many of these are set in Ancient Egypt, or have animal conservation as their theme.

Alain is married with three children and lives in France. Despite writing about the sea in the Jolly Roger series of novels, he rarely sets foot in it, preferring life in the mountains.

ABOUT THE ILLUSTRATOR

Annette Marnat loved drawing as a child, and went on to study illustration in Lyon, France, where she still lives. When she graduated in 2004, her work was selected for the Bologna Children's Book Fair Illustrators catalogue, and commissions from publishers soon followed. She is now a well-established and popular children's book illustrator.

CONTENTS